Nicole
the Beach
Fairy

Special thanks to Narinder Dhami

No part of this publication may be reproduced, stored in a retrieval system, or transmitted in any form or by any means, electronic, mechanical, photocopying, recording, or otherwise, without written permission of the publisher. For information regarding permission, write to Rainbow Magic Limited, c/o HIT Entertainment, 830 South Greenville Avenue, Allen, TX 75002-3320.

ISBN 978-0-545-60524-3

12 11 10 9 8 7 6 5 4 3 2 1   14 15 16 17 18 19/0

Printed in the U.S.A.   40

This edition first printing, July 2014

Nicole

the Beach Fairy

by Daisy Meadows

SCHOLASTIC INC.

The Earth Fairies must be dreaming
If they think they can escape my scheming.
My goblins are by far the greenest,
And I am definitely the meanest.

Seven fairies out to save the earth?
This very idea fills me with mirth!
I'm sure the world has had enough
Of fairy magic and all that stuff.

So I'm going to steal the fairies' wands
And send them into human lands.
The fairies will think all is lost,
Defeated again—by me, Jack Frost!

Contents

Time for Action

"Isn't it wonderful to be back on Rainspell Island again, Rachel?" Kirsty Tate said happily, gazing out over the shimmering blue-green sea. "It hasn't changed a bit!"

Rachel Walker, Kirsty's best friend, nodded. "Rainspell is still as beautiful as ever," she replied as the two girls followed the rocky path down to the beach. "This is one of the most special places in the whole world!"

The Tates and the Walkers were spending school break on Rainspell Island. Even though it was fall, the sky was a clear blue and the sun was shining brightly, so it felt more like summer. Kirsty and Rachel couldn't wait to get to the beach and dip their toes in the ocean.

"You're right, Rachel," Kirsty agreed, her eyes twinkling.  "After all, this is where we first became friends!"

"And we found lots of other amazing friends here, too, didn't we?" Rachel laughed.

Kirsty and Rachel shared a magical secret. During their first visit to Rainspell Island, they'd met the Rainbow Fairies, who had been cast out of Fairyland by Jack Frost's wicked spell. Since then, the girls had gotten to know many of the other fairies. Their tiny, magical friends asked Rachel and Kirsty for help whenever Jack Frost and his goblins were causing trouble.

"This is gorgeous!" Kirsty said as they finally reached the beach.

The golden sand seemed

to stretch for miles into the distance.
Seagulls soared in the sky, and Kirsty
could smell the fresh, salty sea air.
"Should we explore the rock pools?" she
suggested.

But Rachel didn't reply. She was
looking down the beach, her face
clouded with dismay.

"Haven't you noticed
the litter, Kirsty?"
she asked, pointing
ahead of them.

Kirsty stared at
the golden sand
more closely. To her
horror, down near the
water's edge, she could see
some plastic bags blowing
around in the breeze. There were

also some soda cans and empty water bottles floating in the ocean.

"Oh, Rachel, this is awful!" Kirsty exclaimed. "I don't remember seeing *any* litter last time we were here."

Rachel frowned. "We've been learning about the environment and being green at school," she told Kirsty. "And our teacher says that plastic is one of the most dangerous things for sea creatures, because it can kill them if they swallow it or get tangled up in it."

Kirsty shaded her eyes and looked farther down the beach. She could see even more litter strewn across the sand.

"Rachel, we have to do something about this." Kirsty had a determined look on her face. "Rainspell Island is beautiful, and we have to keep it that way. We'll need help, though — and I know just where we can get it!"

Rachel's face lit up. "Fairyland!" she burst out excitedly.

Kirsty nodded. Quickly, the girls opened the magical lockets they wore around their necks. They each took out a pinch of fairy dust.

Rachel and Kirsty sprinkled the
dust over themselves, and instantly
they were surrounded by a mist of
rainbow-colored sparkles that lifted
them off their feet. The two girls spun
through the air, shrinking down to
fairy-size.

A few seconds later, Kirsty and Rachel tumbled gently onto the emerald lawn outside the pink and white Fairyland Palace. To the girls' delight, they saw that the king and queen of Fairyland and their frog footman, Bertram, were already waiting for them.

"Hello, girls," Queen Titania called with a welcoming smile. "We knew that you were on your way!"

"Sorry to turn up so unexpectedly, Your Majesties," Rachel said. "But this time we need *your* help!" Kirsty added.

"You're always welcome in Fairyland, girls," Queen Titania replied with a sweet smile. "You are our dearest friends!"

"Now, how can we help you?" asked King Oberon.

Rachel took a deep breath. "Well, it's about Rainspell Island," she began.

Quickly, Rachel explained how she and Kirsty had found lots of litter on the beach.

"And it's not just Rainspell Island," Kirsty added. "The whole human world needs help with the environment."

The king and queen looked dismayed.

"We've heard about these problems," King Oberon said with a sigh. "But even though we'd like to help, our magic isn't powerful enough to fix them all."

Queen Titania whispered something in the king's ear, and the two of them talked for a moment in low voices. Then the queen turned to Rachel and Kirsty.

"Girls, we have a plan!" she announced. "Today is the Fairyland Wand Ceremony — and you're invited to join us." She turned to Bertram. "Please tell the seven fairies currently in training to meet us immediately by the Seeing Pool."

As Bertram hopped away, Kirsty turned to Rachel.

"The Fairyland Wand Ceremony?" Kirsty whispered, looking very curious. "I wonder what *that* is?"

Meet the Earth Fairies!

Rachel and Kirsty followed the king and queen through the beautiful palace gardens, winding their way between the colorful flowerbeds.

"You're going to meet our seven fairies-in-training," King Oberon explained. "They're at the end of their course in fairy magic, but they haven't taken their final exam yet."

As they got closer to the Seeing Pool, Kirsty and Rachel saw seven pretty fairies waiting for them.

"Look, this must be Rachel and Kirsty!" one of the fairies cried, and all seven of them twirled up into the air.

"Hello! Hello!" they called excitedly as they fluttered around the girls.

"Rachel and Kirsty, meet Nicole, Isabella, Edie, Coral, Lily, Milly, and Carrie," the queen announced. Then she beckoned to the fairies, who landed beside her. "Listen carefully," the queen went on, looking around at them. "The king and I have decided that, just for a trial period, you seven fairies will be given a very special task."

"You're going to become the Earth Fairies!" King Oberon explained. "You'll be helping Rachel and Kirsty clean up the environment in the human world."

All the fairies gasped, clapping their hands with delight. Rachel and Kirsty glanced excitedly at each other.

"If this is successful, then you'll keep your titles as the Earth Fairies," Queen Titania added. "Bertram — the wands, please."

Bertram hopped forward, carrying a tray holding seven glittering wands. But Rachel and Kirsty could see that the wands weren't quite as sparkly as all the others they'd seen before.

"The wands won't be full of magic until the fairies pass their final exam," the king told the girls when he noticed them staring at the tray.

The queen reached for the first wand. "The Seeing Pool will match each fairy to her special assignment," she said with a smile. Then she touched the wand to the smooth, glassy surface of the Seeing Pool.

Immediately, tiny ripples began to spread across the water. The ripples grew bigger and bigger until a picture appeared.

"It's the beach at Rainspell Island!" Kirsty exclaimed.

The queen turned to the first fairy, who was peering into the Seeing Pool. She had blond hair tied in a ponytail, and she wore a red T-shirt, a pink and orange skirt decorated with shells, and flip-flops.

"Nicole, you are the Beach Fairy!" the queen declared, replacing the wand on the tray.

"Yes, Your Majesty," Nicole replied with a big smile.

One by one, the queen touched the remaining wands to the Seeing Pool, calling out each fairy's special task as she did.

"Air for Isabella, Garden for Edie, Reef for Coral, Rain Forest for Lily, River for Milly, and Snow Cap for Carrie."

The fairies looked very excited now.

"The Earth Fairies won't be able to cure the environmental problems in the human world," Queen Titania explained, "since that is the responsibility of *all* creatures on the earth, especially humans." She smiled at Rachel and Kirsty. "But they'll help as much as they can."

"That's fantastic!" Rachel said, thrilled, and Kirsty nodded eagerly.

The king stepped forward.

"It's time for the Fairyland Wand Ceremony," he proclaimed. "Each fairy will now be presented with her wand —"

Suddenly, a gust of icy wind swept through the palace gardens, chilling everyone to the bone. Rachel and Kirsty yelped as they spotted a tall, thin figure zipping straight toward them, riding on the frosty blast. He was surrounded by seven cackling green goblins.

"Oh, no!" Rachel cried. "It's Jack Frost!"

The Goblins Go Green!

Jack Frost zoomed down to the ground with a cold sneer on his face. He snapped his icy fingers. Immediately, the goblins rushed over to Bertram. The frog footman tried to shield the tray from them, but it was no use. The goblins circled him and grabbed the Earth Fairies' wands with hoots of glee.

"Stop that!" the king shouted.

Jack Frost ignored him. Instead, he pointed his own wand at the goblins and sent an ice bolt shooting toward them. The next second, the goblins and the wands vanished in a flurry of snowflakes.

Spinning around, Jack Frost aimed another ice bolt at the Seeing Pool. It shot into the water with a splash, freezing the whole pool on contact.

Jack Frost burst out laughing. "That's better!" he yelled triumphantly. "Earth

Fairies? There are too many fairies
buzzing around here already!
The world doesn't need any more
do-gooders —"

"We're just
trying to be
green," Kirsty
spoke up bravely.

"Green?" Jack
Frost snorted in
disgust. "Being green
isn't that hard — goblins do
it without even thinking!"

"Kirsty means that we're trying to help
the human world become a cleaner and
better place to live," the king said sternly.
"This has nothing to do with you, Jack
Frost. Please give the wands back
immediately."

25

Smirking, Jack Frost put his hands on his hips. "Oh, but I want to help the human world as much as you do," he sneered. "And I know that each fairy wand will lead the goblins to the Earth Fairies' special places." He chuckled. "I'm sure my goblins will give a whole new meaning to the phrase *being green*!"

Before anyone could speak, Jack Frost was gone, soaring away on another frosty blast.

"Oh, no!" Rachel said, looking upset. "Jack Frost and his goblins are going to make things even worse for the environment!"

"Rachel's right," Queen Titania said anxiously. "We simply can't have the goblins running around the human world with fairy wands! No one can *ever* find out about Fairyland."

"And we want our wands back!" Nicole added, looking annoyed. The other fairies murmured in agreement.

"We all have to work together," Kirsty suggested. "We can look for the wands and help the environment at the same time." The seven fairies nodded eagerly. "Remember, Earth Fairies, your magic will be limited because you're still in training," the king reminded them. "But your wands will give you a magical boost if you can get them back from the goblins."

"The goblin with my wand will be at the beach on Rainspell Island, because that was my assignment," Nicole said. "Let's go there right away!" She linked hands with Rachel and Kirsty.

"Good luck!" the other fairies cried.

The queen lifted her wand. A shower of dazzling fairy dust surrounded Rachel, Kirsty, and Nicole for a moment before it swept them away.

Seagull in Distress

As the mist of glittering sparkles cleared, the girls landed on the Rainspell Island beach. They were human-size again!

"We'd better find the goblin as fast as we can," said Nicole, who was hovering above them. "He must be on the beach somewhere."

"Let's start walking," Kirsty suggested. "There's a lot of ground to cover!"

As they headed down the golden
stretch of sand, Nicole noticed the bits of
litter strewn around the beach. Her eyes
grew wide.

"Girls, I see what
you mean!" she
exclaimed as
Kirsty bent to
pick up an empty
soda can.

"Let's collect as
much litter as we can,"
Rachel suggested, scooping up a plastic
bottle.

Nicole and the girls moved down the
beach, searching for the goblin. But
before long, Rachel and Kirsty both had
too much litter to carry, and there were
no garbage or recycling bins anywhere.

"I don't have much magic without my wand, but I should be able to help," Nicole said. She snapped her fingers and a tiny shower of sparkles burst around the girls. The next moment, two glittery bags appeared at Rachel's and Kirsty's feet, one for recycling and one for trash.

"Thanks, Nicole," Kirsty said gratefully. She and Rachel put the litter they'd collected into the bags and continued along the beach. The fairy flew next to them, swooping down to pick up candy wrappers.

A few minutes later, the girls spotted a family sitting on the beach ahead of them. A mom, a dad, a little girl, and her younger brother were having a picnic. Nicole immediately ducked out of sight behind Kirsty's hair.

As Rachel and Kirsty passed by, the little girl and her brother jumped to their feet and ran over to them.

"What are you doing?" the little girl asked shyly.

"We're trying to clean up the beach," Rachel explained with a smile.

"Don't you think it would look nicer without all this garbage lying around?" Kirsty asked.

The boy and girl nodded.

"We can help!" they cried excitedly.
They ran over to their parents and came
back with their hands full of sandwich
bags and empty
drink cartons.
Rachel opened
the sacks, and
they dropped
the garbage
inside.

"If everyone did
that, the beach would be cleaned up in
no time!" Kirsty said with a laugh.

"We'll always clean up after our picnics
from now on," the little girl promised
solemnly.

"Let's go and tell Mom and Dad," the
boy said eagerly, and they ran off.

Rachel and Kirsty grinned.

"Good job, girls!" Nicole whispered, flitting out to sit on Kirsty's shoulder. "You're already getting people to think about cleaning up after themselves!"

The girls walked on, filling their bags as they went. Suddenly, they all jumped as they heard a loud, ear-splitting screech.

"What was that?" Kirsty asked.

"Look!" Rachel gasped, pointing to the water's edge.

A large white seagull was flapping around on the sand. He had a plastic bag tangled around his feet, and he was tearing at it with his yellow beak, trying to get free.

"Quick, girls!" Nicole said as the seagull screeched again in panic. "We have to help him."

Rachel and Kirsty dashed over to the seagull, with Nicole zooming alongside them.

"Hello!" Nicole called, fluttering down to hover near the frightened bird. "I'm Nicole, and these are my friends Rachel and Kirsty. Don't worry, they'll set you free!"

"That's awfully nice of you," the seagull panted as the girls kneeled down on the sand beside him. He stopped flapping his wings and

sat quietly while Rachel and Kirsty
gently untangled the plastic bag.

"There you go!" Rachel said as they
finally freed him. The seagull gave
a screech of relief and hopped happily
around the sand. Meanwhile, Kirsty
shoved the plastic bag in with the rest of
the recycling.

"Thank
you," the
seagull
said.
"My
name is
Screech, if
you haven't
already
guessed!"

Rachel, Kirsty, and Nicole laughed.

"Pleased to meet you, Screech," they all said.

"Isn't this garbage awful?" Screech complained, looking around the beach. "I'm not the only sea creature who's getting tangled up in it, you know. Lots of other birds and animals are suffering, too. And not just on this beach, but on other beaches around the mainland."

Nicole's eyes opened wide.

"So *that's* what my special assignment is really about!" she exclaimed. "When I get my wand back, I'm going to help clean up *all* beaches."

"Look how much garbage we've

collected already!" Kirsty said to
Screech, showing him her recycling bag.

"Can I help?" Screech asked eagerly.

Before Kirsty could reply, there was a
flapping of wings overhead. The girls
glanced up and saw another seagull
swooping down toward them.

"Hi, Screech!" the gull called. "Do you want to come and play? Bet I can catch more fish than you can!"

"Not today, Beaky," Screech called back. "I'm going to stay with my new friends, Nicole, Kirsty, and Rachel, and help them pick up garbage."

Beaky looked disappointed. "Everyone seems to be picking up garbage today," he remarked.

"What do you mean?" Rachel asked curiously.

"Well, I saw a little green man picking up garbage and throwing it into the sea," Beaky replied. "He was farther down the beach." The seagull pointed with his wing.

Kirsty gasped. "It must be a goblin!"

Goblin with a Wand

"Thanks, Beaky!" Nicole cried. "Come on, girls!"

Rachel and Kirsty raced down the beach, with Screech and Nicole flying along behind them. After a few minutes they could see a small figure ahead in the distance.

"There's the goblin," Nicole whispered. "And he has my wand!"

The goblin was standing by the water's edge, the wand tucked firmly under his arm. He had a pile of garbage near his feet. As Nicole, Rachel, Kirsty, and Screech came closer, he picked up an empty water bottle and tossed it into the ocean.

"What are you doing?" Kirsty called, annoyed.

The goblin spun around. He scowled when he saw them, and immediately hid the wand behind his back.

"I'm just trying to be green!" he retorted. With that, he kicked a soda can into the waves.

"But you're not helping the environment at all!" Rachel pointed out. "Throwing garbage into the ocean just makes the water polluted."

"Anyway, the tide will probably bring the garbage right back in," Kirsty added. "It will end up on this beach again, or on another beach somewhere else."

The goblin looked confused. "You're lying!" he said accusingly.

"It's true!" Kirsty insisted.

"Please give the wand back to Nicole," Rachel urged. "Then she can use it to help the environment the right way."

"No way!" the goblin roared furiously.

"The wand is mine — Jack Frost said so!" He waved it at them menacingly.

Rachel and Kirsty took a step backward, feeling nervous.

"What kind of magic can a goblin do with a fairy's wand?" Kirsty whispered to Nicole.

"I don't really know." Nicole frowned. "These wands are new, and have never been used before. The magic in each wand is meant for only one fairy — and I have no idea what will happen if someone else tries to use it!"

They all stared at the goblin. He was crumpling up candy wrappers into a ball. Then he threw the ball into the air and hit it with the wand, using the wand like a baseball bat! The ball of garbage  sailed through the air, landing in the water with a splash, and the goblin chuckled with glee.

"We have to get the wand back — and fast!" Rachel said to her friends. "Maybe Screech can help us." She glanced at the seagull. "Do you feel up to it after what happened with the plastic bag?"

"I'm much better now," Screech replied. "I'd be happy to help."

"Maybe you could fly around the goblin and try to snatch the wand from him," Kirsty suggested.

Screech nodded. "I'll do my best!"

Nicole and the girls watched hopefully as the seagull soared through the air toward the goblin.

"Go away!" the goblin shrieked as Screech hovered above him. But the seagull grabbed the tip of the wand in his

beak, and tried to tug it out of the
goblin's hand.

"Let go!" the goblin bellowed, yanking
the wand free. "Get your own wand,
you annoying bird! This one's mine!"

Circling overhead, Screech tried to

grab the wand
again and
again. But
the goblin
was hanging
on to it tightly,
with both hands.
He even began lashing
out at the seagull with it.

"Screech looks tired," Rachel said
anxiously, after a few minutes. The
seagull's wings were moving much more
slowly now. "I think he should stop."

"Come back, Screech," Nicole called.
Screech flew over to them, looking
disappointed.

"I'm so sorry," he said. "You helped me,
but I couldn't get the wand back for you."

"Thanks for trying," Kirsty told him.
"Now you should go home and rest.
You look tired!"

"I am," Screech confessed. "It isn't
every day I get tangled up in a plastic
bag and meet a fairy, a
goblin, *and* two human
girls!" Flapping a wing
in farewell, he flew off.

The goblin whirled
the wand triumphantly
over his head.

"Ha, ha! Can't
catch me!" he taunted

Nicole and the girls. "Now go away —
or I'm going to zap you with my wand!"
The goblin frowned. "Just as soon as I
figure out how to use it," he mumbled to
himself.

"We're not moving until we get the
wand back," Rachel said firmly.

"Well, I'm definitely going to zap you,
then!" the goblin retorted. He began
waving the wand around wildly, trying
to get the magic to work.

Nicole looked annoyed. "A fairy's wand
shouldn't be used to hurt anyone," she
said. "It should only be used for good
magic, and to change people into fairies."

Suddenly, Kirsty's eyes widened. Nicole
had just given her a great idea!

A Little Human Magic!

"Rachel, you and I need to shrink
to fairy-size again," Kirsty whispered.

"Can I help?" Nicole asked shyly. "I've
never tried shrinking anyone before, but
I think I can do it."

"Sure," the girls agreed. They trusted
their fairy friend!

Nicole waved her tiny hands and a

few sparkles of fairy dust floated down
around Kirsty and Rachel.

The girls began to shrink until they
were the same size as Nicole, with
beautiful, shimmering
wings on their backs.

"Nice work,
Nicole!"
they
cheered.

"Now
just follow
my lead,"
Kirsty said. She
flew over to the
goblin, with Nicole
and Rachel close
behind.

"Look at us!" Kirsty shouted,

hovering above the goblin's head. "You
might have the wand, but we can *fly*!"

"So? That's no big deal," the goblin
said grumpily. "I could
be a mean, green,
flying machine if I
wanted." He shut his
eyes tightly and
tapped himself on
the head with the
wand. Nicole,
Rachel, and Kirsty
saw a faint mist of
fairy dust swirl out
of the tip.

"Anything happen
yet?" the goblin called.

"No!" Nicole and the girls
yelled back, trying not to laugh.

Frowning, the goblin opened his eyes and whirled the wand through the air very quickly. There was a sudden burst of glitter, and the goblin began to

shrink. A moment later, a pretty pair of translucent wings appeared on his back. "Yes!" The goblin laughed triumphantly as he zoomed up into the air. "I can fly just like you!"

"And now we just need to get him so dizzy that he drops the wand!" Kirsty whispered, winking at Nicole and Rachel.

The goblin was still getting used to his new wings. He darted clumsily through

the air, stopping and starting and almost
losing control. Then he tumbled back
down toward the beach, but managed to
swoop up into the air again before he hit
the sand.

"OK, so you can fly," Kirsty called as
the goblin finally began to float around
in slow, lazy circles. "But can you
loop the loop?"

Kirsty dashed through the
air, completing four
loops all in a row.

The goblin
scowled. "Of
course I can!"
He flew through
the air like
Kirsty had, but
only managed

to complete three loops. Then he spun
out of control and somersaulted head
over heels in midair.

"What about this?" Rachel asked,
before the goblin had time to
recover. She began doing
backflips, then zipping
around in circles. The
goblin copied her with
a determined look
on his face.

"Or this?"
Nicole said,
flying backward in
a zigzag pattern.

The girls and
Nicole were all
swooping and zooming
through the air, leaving sparkly trails of

fairy dust behind them like a fireworks
display. The goblin looked a bit dazed
as he tried to keep up with them. He
was zigzagging along in a very wobbly
way now.

"Let's go for it!" Kirsty
whispered to Nicole and
Rachel.

With that, the
three friends began
to weave a fast,
complicated pattern of
big circles in the air,
zooming around and
around. The goblin
tried to join in, but it
was all too much for him.

"I'm too dizzy!" he complained. With
a groan, he closed his eyes. Then he

plummeted down toward the sand and landed with a *thud*. The wand flew out of his hand.

"Thank you!" Nicole said, swooping down to pick up the wand.

Rachel and Kirsty saw the wand begin to twinkle and glow with fairy magic. As the goblin opened his eyes, Nicole pointed the wand at him. A burst of magic dust made the goblin grow to his usual size, and his fairy wings disappeared. He looked very annoyed.

"Now you need to go back to Fairyland," Nicole told him.

Angrily, the goblin jumped to his feet.

"Horrible fairies!" he muttered, brushing the sand off. "You might have the wand, but you'll *never* be as green as me!"

As he stomped away, Kirsty, Rachel, and Nicole laughed.

"Thank you so much, girls," said Nicole as another shower of sparkles from her wand made Rachel and Kirsty human-size again. "Now I can do my job, helping to clean up beaches everywhere."

Nicole waved her wand in the air again, and four more sparkly recycling bags appeared. "Here you go, girls," she said, glancing down the beach. "You have plenty more work to do here!"

Rachel and Kirsty both sighed as they stared at all the litter lying around.

"Yes, but there are only two of us," Rachel pointed out.

Nicole smiled. "You know what?" she said with a wink. "You have your very own magic to help you! Now I'm off to Fairyland to give everyone the good news."

She vanished in a cloud of fairy magic.

Rachel and Kirsty looked at each other in confusion.

"Our own magic?" Kirsty repeated, opening one of the new bags. "What did Nicole mean, Rachel?"

Rachel was smiling. "I think I know!" she replied, pointing up the beach.

Kirsty saw four people coming toward them — their parents.

"Mom! Dad!" Rachel called, waving at Mr. and Mrs. Walker. "Will you help me and Kirsty collect litter?"

"If everyone helps, it won't take long at all," Kirsty pointed out.

"We'll *all* help," said Mrs. Tate as they joined the girls. "We were just talking about how awful it looks."

"And how dangerous it is for all the sea creatures," Mr. Tate added. "Hand me a bag, Rachel."

"Let's come to the beach every morning we're here and pick up garbage, Rachel," Kirsty suggested as all six of them headed down the beach with their recycling bags.

"Great idea," Rachel agreed.

"Cleaning up the beach would go even faster if we got more people involved," Mrs. Tate said thoughtfully. "Why don't I make some flyers to ask other people for help?"

"I'll hand out the flyers," Mr. Walker offered. "And maybe we can organize a group of volunteers to clean up the beach year-round."

Rachel and Kirsty beamed at each other.

"Maybe we *can* make a difference," Kirsty said happily.

"All it takes is a little human magic!" Rachel replied with a laugh.

Nicole the Beach Fairy has her wand back!
Now Rachel and Kirsty need to help

the Air Fairy!

Join their next adventure
in this special sneak peek. . . .

Flower Fairy

"Rachel! Kirsty! Hurry up, we need to go!" came a voice from downstairs. "Coming, Mom!" Kirsty Tate shouted back, putting her hair in a ponytail. "There," she said. "Are you ready, Rachel?"

Rachel Walker, Kirsty's best friend, frowned as she gazed around the bedroom the two girls were sharing. "Almost," she said. "But I don't know where my shoes are. Have you seen them?"

Kirsty shook her head. "Maybe they're in the hall," she suggested.

The girls hurried down to find their parents waiting by the front door. The two families were staying in a cottage together for a week on Rainspell Island. It was a very magical place, as Kirsty and Rachel had discovered the first time they'd been there on vacation. That would always be a summer to remember: Not only had they met each other, but they'd also met some very special fairy friends!

So far, this vacation was proving to be just as exciting. They had only arrived yesterday, but Rachel and Kirsty had already found themselves in another wonderful fairy adventure. This time, they were helping the Earth Fairies with a mission to clean up the world's environmental problems.

Today, the two families were going to Seabury, a town on the mainland. The girls wanted to go to a movie and the grownups were going shopping. Kirsty and Rachel really hoped they'd meet another fairy at some point!

Mr. Walker looked at his watch. "Girls, we have to leave now if you're going to make it in time for the movie. The ferry to the mainland leaves in ten minutes, and there won't be another one for an hour."

"I can't find my shoes, Dad," Rachel said, hunting all around the hallway closet. "Where could they be?"

Kirsty helped her look, and the girls searched the entire cottage before finally finding the shoes under Rachel's bed.

"At last," said Mr. Tate when they reappeared. "We'll have to drive to the ferry now. There isn't time to walk. We're cutting it close as it is."

RAINBOW magic™

Which Magical Fairies Have You Met?

- ❏ The Rainbow Fairies
- ❏ The Weather Fairies
- ❏ The Jewel Fairies
- ❏ The Pet Fairies
- ❏ The Dance Fairies
- ❏ The Music Fairies
- ❏ The Sports Fairies
- ❏ The Party Fairies
- ❏ The Ocean Fairies
- ❏ The Night Fairies
- ❏ The Magical Animal Fairies
- ❏ The Princess Fairies
- ❏ The Superstar Fairies
- ❏ The Fashion Fairies
- ❏ The Sugar & Spice Fairies

■ SCHOLASTIC

Find all of your favorite fairy friends at
scholastic.com/rainbowmagic

HIT entertainment

RMFAIRY9

RAINBOW magic

These activities are magical!
Play dress-up, send friendship notes,
and much more!

SCHOLASTIC
www.scholastic.com
www.rainbowmagiconline.com

HiT entertainment

RMACTIV3

RAINBOW magic™

SPECIAL EDITION

Which Magical Fairies Have You Met?

3 stories in each one!

- ❑ Joy the Summer Vacation Fairy
- ❑ Holly the Christmas Fairy
- ❑ Kylie the Carnival Fairy
- ❑ Stella the Star Fairy
- ❑ Shannon the Ocean Fairy
- ❑ Trixie the Halloween Fairy
- ❑ Gabriella the Snow Kingdom Fairy
- ❑ Juliet the Valentine Fairy
- ❑ Mia the Bridesmaid Fairy
- ❑ Flora the Dress-Up Fairy
- ❑ Paige the Christmas Play Fairy
- ❑ Emma the Easter Fairy
- ❑ Cara the Camp Fairy
- ❑ Destiny the Rock Star Fairy
- ❑ Belle the Birthday Fairy
- ❑ Olympia the Games Fairy
- ❑ Selena the Sleepover Fairy
- ❑ Cheryl the Christmas Tree Fairy
- ❑ Florence the Friendship Fairy
- ❑ Lindsay the Luck Fairy
- ❑ Brianna the Tooth Fairy
- ❑ Autumn the Falling Leaves Fairy
- ❑ Keira the Movie Star Fairy
- ❑ Addison the April Fool's Day Fairy

▌▌SCHOLASTIC

Find all of your favorite fairy friends at
scholastic.com/rainbowmagic

HIT entertainment

RMSPECIAL12